It was cool and damp on the riverbank –
just right for a little turtle.

"I'm hungry," said Little Turtle.

He went to find something to eat.

3

Little Turtle walked away from the river.

He found lots of things to eat.

But he forgot that the riverbank

was just right for a little turtle.

Little Turtle
and the Coyote

by Damian Harvey and
Richard Watson

W
FRANKLIN WATTS
LONDON•SYDNEY

The sun was coming up.

Little Turtle climbed out of the river and onto the bank.

Little Turtle forgot that the river helped him stay damp and cool. He forgot that if turtles get too dry, they cannot walk.

Little Turtle also forgot what happens when the sun comes up.

The sun shone down on Little Turtle.

It climbed higher and higher in the sky.

Little Turtle started to feel very hot.

"I need to go back to the river where it's nice and cool," said Little Turtle. He turned around and started to walk back to the river.

But Little Turtle got hotter and hotter.

Soon he had to stop.

"I can't walk," he said.

"I'm too hot!"

He found a hole and went inside.

It was cool and damp in the hole.

"I can't get back to the river,"

said Little Turtle, and he began to cry.

Coyote came along. He heard
Little Turtle's cries. He thought
it was somebody singing.
"What beautiful singing," said Coyote.
"I want to sing like that."

Coyote looked into the hole.

He saw Little Turtle crying.

"I want to sing like you," said Coyote.

"Please will you teach me?"

"I wasn't singing," said Little Turtle.

"You were," said Coyote. "I heard you."

Coyote got cross.

"Teach me your song," he said,

"or I will eat you up in one gulp."

"You can't eat me," said Little Turtle.

"My shell will hurt you."

"Then I will throw you out
in the hot sun," said Coyote.
"The sun won't hurt me,"
said Little Turtle. "I will hide in my shell
until it gets dark."

Coyote got crosser and crosser.
"Teach me your song," he said,
"or I will throw you in the river."
Coyote did not know that the river
was just right for a little turtle.
Turtle made a plan to stay safe.

"Please don't throw me in the river," said Little Turtle.

Coyote laughed. He picked up Little Turtle in his mouth.

He took him back to the river and threw him in.

Little Turtle stuck his head up
out of the water.

"Thank you, Coyote," said Little Turtle.

"You have helped me get back
to the river."

Little Turtle had tricked Coyote.

Coyote growled angrily

and walked away.

Story order

Look at these 5 pictures and captions.
Put the pictures in the right order
to retell the story.

1

Coyote threw Little Turtle in the river.

2

Little Turtle climbed out of the river.

3

Little Turtle found lots to eat.

4

Coyote heard Little Turtle.

5

Little Turtle hid in a hole.

Guide for Independent Reading

This series is designed to provide an opportunity for your child to read on their own. These notes are written for you to help your child choose a book and to read it independently.

In school, your child's teacher will often be using reading books which have been banded to support the process of learning to read. Use the book band colour your child is reading in school to help you make a good choice. *Little Turtle and the Coyote* is a good choice for children reading at Turquoise Band in their classroom to read independently. The aim of independent reading is to read this book with ease, so that your child enjoys the story and relates it to their own experiences.

About the book
In this North American tale, Little Turtle wanders too far from the river and tricks Coyote into taking him home.

Before reading
Help your child to learn how to make good choices by asking: "Why did you choose this book? Why do you think you will enjoy it?" Look at the cover together and ask: "What do you think the story will be about?" Ask your child to think of what they already know about the story context. Then ask your child to read the title aloud. Ask: "What do you think Little Turtle will be doing in the story?" Remind your child that they can sound out a word in syllable chunks if they get stuck.

Decide together whether your child will read the story independently or read it aloud to you.

During reading

Remind your child of what they know and what they can do independently. If reading aloud, support your child if they hesitate or ask for help by telling them the word. If reading to themselves, remind your child that they can come and ask for your help if stuck.

After reading

Support comprehension by asking your child to tell you about the story. Use the story order puzzle to encourage your child to retell the story in the right sequence, in their own words. The correct sequence can be found on the next page.

Help your child think about the messages in the book that go beyond the story and ask: "Do you think Little Turtle and Coyote could become friends? Will Little Turtle wander too far from the river again?"

Give your child a chance to respond to the story: "Did you have a favourite part? What did you think would happen when Coyote picked up Little Turtle?"

Extending learning

Help your child understand the story structure by using the same sentence patterning and adding different elements. "Let's make up a new story about animals tricking each other. What animals will we choose? What trick could your animals play?"

In the classroom, your child's teacher may be teaching about recognising punctuation marks. Ask your child to identify speech marks in the story and look at how they are used to show when a character is speaking.

Franklin Watts
First published in Great Britain in 2022
by Hodder & Stoughton

Copyright © Hodder & Stoughton Limited, 2022

Series Editors: Jackie Hamley and Melanie Palmer
Series Advisors and Development Editors: Dr Sue Bodman and Glen Franklin
Series Designers: Cathryn Gilbert and Peter Scoulding

A CIP catalogue record for this book is
available from the British Library.

ISBN 978 1 4451 8413 5 (hbk)
ISBN 978 1 4451 8414 2 (pbk)
ISBN 978 1 4451 8495 1 (library ebook)
ISBN 978 1 4451 8494 4 (ebook)

Printed in China

Franklin Watts
An imprint of
Hachette Children's Group
Part of Hodder & Stoughton
Carmelite House
50 Victoria Embankment
London EC4Y 0DZ

An Hachette UK Company
www.hachette.co.uk

www.reading-champion.co.uk

Answer to Story order: 2, 3, 5, 4, 1